# THE NINE FURRY PURRY BEANCAT

THE RAILWAY CAT

## PHILIP ARDAGH

Illustrated by

*Rob Biddulph*

SIMON & SCHUSTER

First published in Great Britain in 2020 by Simon & Schuster UK Ltd

Text Copyright © 2020 Philip Ardagh
Illustrations Copyright © 2020 Rob Biddulph

1 3 5 7 9 10 8 6 4 2

Simon & Schuster UK Ltd
1st Floor, 222 Gray's Inn Road
London
WC1X 8HB

www.simonandschuster.co.uk
www.simonandschuster.com.au
www.simonandschuster.co.in

Simon & Schuster Australia, Sydney
Simon & Schuster India, New Delhi

A CIP catalogue record for this book is available from the British Library.

PB ISBN 978-1-4711-8403-1
eBook ISBN 978-1-4711-8404-8

Printed and bound by CPI Group (UK) Ltd, Croydon, CR0 4YY

THE ADVENTURES OF

FURRY PURRY

# BEANCAT

THE
RAILWAY
CAT

# PHILIP ARDAGH

Illustrated by
*Rob Biddulph*

More Furry Purry
Beancat adventures!

**THE PIRATE CAPTAIN'S CAT**

**THE LIBRARY CAT –**
coming soon!

This one's for Ginger
Biscuit, my son's
much-loved moggy.
**Philip Ardagh**


For Flo
**Rob Biddulph**

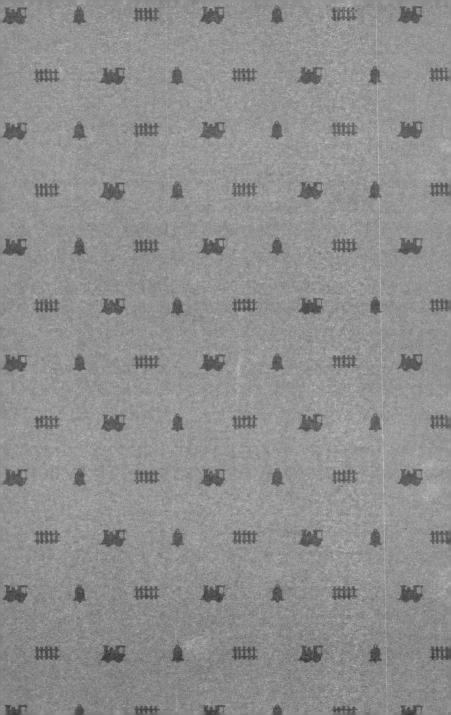

**F**urry Purry Beancat found a patch of sunlight, followed her tail round in a circle three times, then settled herself down in a furry ball of purry cat. She yawned, lowered her head to the ground and pulled her beautiful, fluffy tail in front of her little pink nose.

*Where will I wake up next?* she wondered, slowly closing her big green eyes and drifting off to sleep . . .

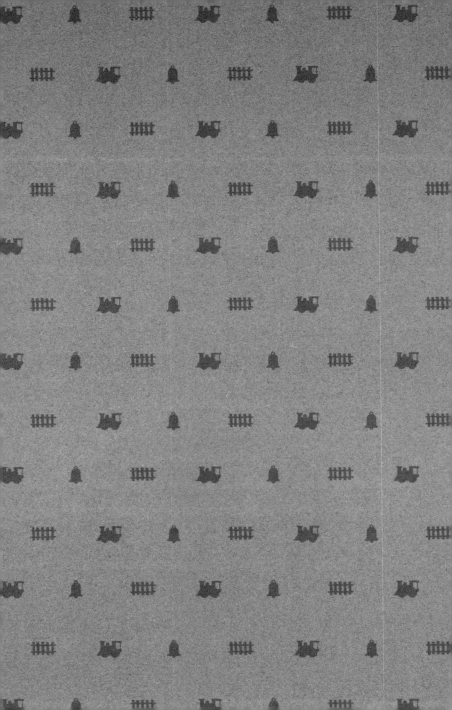

# CHAPTER 1
## 'THIEF!'

**F**urry Purry Beancat was woken by the sound of a steam whistle. She opened her big green eyes to find herself in a cloud of white smoke, her little pink nose filled with the smell of burning coal, engine oil, hot metal and a thousand and one other things.

She rather liked it!

As the smoke cleared, Beancat discovered that she was sitting on a large package wrapped in brown paper and string. This was on top of another package wrapped in brown paper and string on top of ANOTHER, all of which were on some kind of large, flat-bed trolley. She felt a bit like a present under a Christmas tree. But where was she?

You see, Furry Purry Beancat is no ordinary cat. Oh no. Beancat is an *extraordinary* cat because, after one of her special cat-naps, she wakes to find herself somewhere completely different! And every time she wakes up in another one of her nine lives, Beancat knows that an adventure is about to happen . . .

Furry Purry Beancat stood up, streeeeeetched and casually looked around, in the way that all cats do. And then she saw it, the reason for all the smoke. There was a steam engine. She was on a railway platform!

Passengers were climbing on and off the carriages, and clusters of people were either greeting new arrivals or saying fond farewells. Some passengers were struggling with bags on their own. One man had a trunk almost as big as he was. Others were being helped by a tall, thin man in a smart uniform who had a trolley, much smaller and more upright than the one Beancat was sitting on.

'Hello, Tom!' said a passenger, with a wave. 'Busy as ever, I see.'

The man in the uniform smiled. 'That I am, sir,' he said. 'A porter's work is never done!'

*Tom looks friendly,* Furry Purry Beancat decided, only to have her thoughts rudely interrupted.

'Thief!' cried a well-dressed woman with a large nose and an even larger hat covered

in peacock feathers. Heads turned in the woman's direction, including Beancat's, and she watched a boy – who looked no more than nine or so – running full-speed ahead, weaving his way in and out of the people on the platform, clutching what had to be the lady's handbag. A soldier in bright red uniform, about to board the train, reached out to try to catch him, but the lad swerved to avoid his clutches.

*He's fast*, thought Beancat. *I'll give him that!*

Tom abandoned his trolley, lunged forward and grabbed the runaway by the waist, lifting him off the ground, his legs still running but in mid-air.

It might have looked comical, but Furry

Purry Beancat noticed that the boy had no shoes and that his feet were covered in soot and grime.

'Let me go!' cried the boy.

'Drop the bag,' said Tom.

The boy dropped the handbag on to the platform. Now he could lash out with his arms, but the porter was too strong for him, and the pummelling from the boy's clenched fists barely reached its target.

An older man, also in a railway uniform, jumped down from the guard's van at the rear of the train, and ran along the platform to help Tom.

*He must work on the railway too,* thought Beancat. The trouble with waking up in a different one of her nine lives each time was that she had NO memory of having been there before. She didn't know WHERE she was, or even WHAT YEAR it was! Others may know her, but she wouldn't remember them!

Tom gently lowered the boy to the ground. He kept hold of one arm while the older man – who did indeed work for the railway as a train guard – took the other. Although the young thief was only small, the two men were making doubly sure that he wasn't going anywhere.

A man in a brown checked suit and bowler hat bent down and picked up the snatched handbag from the platform. He dusted it down with his hands, made his way over to the woman in the peacock-feathered

hat and handed it back to her. 'There you go, madam,' he said, touching the brim of his hat.

Furry Purry Beancat noticed he had a very impressive moustache. *But not as impressive as my tail*, she thought. And that wasn't ALL she'd noticed.

'Thank you!' said the lady, looking flustered. Her face had gone a funny colour. 'I really am most grateful.' She took her handbag from the man.

'It was young Tom, 'ere, who caught 'im, ma'am,' said the train guard, nodding at the porter.

'It was indeed,' said the lady. 'I saw it all! I am grateful to you, Tom, and to you . . . ?' Her eyes fell on the guard.

'Jim, ma'am,' said the train guard. 'Jim Graves.' He touched the peak of his cap with his free hand, the other still gripping the arm of the boy.

*There's a lot of hat-touching going on around here!* thought Beancat. *It must be a sign of respect. A way of being polite.* She noticed the man with the brown checked suit and bowler hat lose himself among the crowd of onlookers and head towards the exit. *As slippery as an eel*, she thought. *I'll bet he wore that brown checked suit and brown bowler hat on purpose. All people will remember is that and his moustache and nothing else about him. Not his face. Nothing.*

Beancat decided to get closer to the action. There was so much going on that no one paid attention to the beautiful, fluffy tabby-and-white cat as she walked among them, magnificent tail held high, watching with her big green eyes and listening with her tufty ears. (The truth be told, she wasn't used to being so totally ignored in this way!)

She looked with particular interest at the boy. His trousers were a good few sizes too short for him and patched and torn, while his shirt appeared to have been crudely sewn from an odd piece of material. All were as dirty as he was skin and bone.

'Thank you for your assistance, Mr Graves,' said the lady. She looked down at the boy. 'As for you . . .'

'I'm 'ungry!' said the boy.

'That,' said the lady, 'is no excuse. I myself am on the committee for a charity to help the poor, and provision is made for those who work for their supper.'

A small crowd had gathered around them. 'Excuse me, please!' said a voice of authority. Everyone stepped aside as

another man joined the group. He was wearing a smart uniform similar to Tom and Jim's, but Furry Purry Beancat could tell straight away that this man was in charge.

A nice warm feeling passed through Beancat. *Is he my special person in this life?* she wondered. Whichever life she wakes up in, Beancat always seems to find she has a special person. (Unlike dogs, no one ever really *owns* a cat, you see.) Sometimes, it requires a little detective work or a matter of wait-and-see to find out who that person is and, sometimes, Furry Purry Beancat can tell in an instant, with just a look or a feeling. And now she certainly took an instant liking to this man, whoever he was.

He had two silver chains on his waistcoat. The first disappeared into one of its pockets, and Furry Purry Beancat thought she could make out the outline of a pocket watch sitting inside. A silver whistle hung from the other. To top it all off, a greying moustache sat below the man's nose. He looked at Jim and raised an enquiring eyebrow.

'Good afternoon, Mr Robinson, sir,' said Jim. 'This lad 'ere stole this 'ere 'andbag from this 'ere lady, and Tom 'ere stopped him.'

Mr Robinson stared at the boy. 'What do you have to say for yourself, young man?' he said.

'I'm 'ungry!' repeated the boy.

'Of all the people to try to steal from,' said Mr Robinson. 'This is Mrs James Fitzpatrick.' He said the name as if everyone should know who she was.

*James?* thought Furry Purry Beancat. That seems an odd name for a woman.

'Mrs Fitzpatrick is well known for her good works and charitable nature. In truth, I suspect, had you asked her for a ha'penny for food or for a slice of bread, she might have given it to you, generous lady that she is.'

*That doesn't sound like this woman to me,* thought Beancat, peering at the woman. *She may run a charity, but that sour look on her face makes her look as kindly as a bag of rusty nails!*

'Well, I—' began Mrs Fitzpatrick, only to be interrupted by Mr Robinson.

'What is your name, boy?'

'Charlie, sir. Charlie Gruff.'

'Well, Charlie, what are we to do with you? My first instinct is, of course, to call for the police.'

*Really?* thought Beancat. *Hmmm. I'm not so sure! I think Mr Robinson must be up to something . . .*

Mrs Fitzpatrick adjusted her returned handbag upon her arm. 'An excelle—'

'But I'm sure Mrs Fitzpatrick would have something to say about that,' added Mr Robinson, before the lady in question could get the chance to say something about *anything*. 'I have absolutely no doubt that she will insist we give you a second chance; and perhaps ask us if we might do the same.'

Beancat could see that the train guard and the porter were doing their best not to smile.

'Mr Robinson—' began Mrs Fitzpatrick.

Mr Robinson raised his hand, 'No, madam. I shall follow your example and deal with this serious matter without involving the police. If only everyone was as kind and understanding as you. You are an inspiration to us all!'

Mrs Fitzpatrick stopped trying to interrupt and positively glowed.

*If she were a cat*, thought Furry Purry Beancat, *she'd be purring louder than the biggest tomcat!* Beancat LIKED this Mr Robinson!

The man pulled his pocket watch from his pocket – where else! – and checked the time. 'Back to your posts, please. This train was due to leave three minutes ago. Charlie Gruff, you can come with me.' He took the boy by the arm.

Beancat was fascinated. For one, she had

noticed something that no one else had. Between picking up the snatched handbag, dusting it down and handing it back to Mrs Fitzpatrick, the man in the brown checked suit and brown bowler hat had slipped a small suede-leather pouch out of it. He'd done it so smoothly and with such lightning speed, it was obvious that he was very skilled at such actions and must have done something similar many times before.

Maybe he and Charlie Gruff were working together or – more likely – Charlie was *working for Brown Bowler.*

*So what was their plan?* Furry Purry Beancat wondered as she followed Mr Robinson and the boy across the platform. *For Charlie to get away with the bag, if he could, and to act as a decoy – a distraction – if he couldn't? But what if Mr Robinson had called for a policeman? Would Brown Bowler have abandoned Charlie?* If she'd been a dog, Beancat might have tried to find a way to tell the others that this man was a thief, like leaping up at Brown Bowler or biting his trousers.

But, as a cat, what could she do? Store away the information, that's what.

Cats are very good at that in general, and Furry Purry Beancat was very good at that in particular, whichever of her different nine lives she might find herself in. That's often why cats look so knowing or, as some think – and I should lower my voice here – smug!

Beancat followed Mr Robinson and Charlie through a door into the station building itself. Inside, Beancat spotted the window and counter of a ticket office over to her right. There was a man sitting on the other side of the window.

Opposite the ticket office, on the wall to Beancat's left, was a door with a sign that said:

# STATIONMASTER'S OFFICE.

Hanging next to it, above a high-backed wooden bench built into the plastered wall, was a framed photograph of a very stern-looking woman. She looked a bit frightening! At the bottom of the frame was a plaque on which was written:

**QUEEN VICTORIA**

QUEEN OF THE UNITED KINGDOM
OF GREAT BRITAIN & IRELAND
AND EMPRESS OF INDIA

It was then Beancat realized that the only people she had seen working at the station had been men. *Well, they may all be men here,* she thought, *but the person in charge of the whole country seems to be a woman.*

If the queen's title had been any longer, Beancat wouldn't have had time to finish reading it before slipping into the stationmaster's office just as the door closed!

# CHAPTER 2
# UNDER ARREST

**T**he minute they were inside, Mr Robinson let go of Charlie. Beancat was surprised that the boy didn't make a dash for the door and for freedom.

Then she sniffed the air and realized why. She smelled biscuits.

'I'll put the kettle on,' said Mr Robinson

(who Beancat now knew must be the stationmaster), removing his cap and jacket and hanging them on a very large metal hook on the back of the door. 'I expect you'd like a cup of tea.'

'Yes, sir!' said the boy, then added a 'Fank you, sir.'

*What a polite young thief*, thought Beancat.

'Good. And help yourself to a biscuit. Only one, mind.'

The stationmaster left the room to make the tea and Beancat jumped up on to a chair and took in her surroundings.

At the centre of the room was a large mahogany desk. On it was a newspaper opened at a page with a large headline along the top reading: 'WAR BREWING'.

*Hmmm,* thought Beancat. *There's war brewing in the country and the stationmaster is about to brew tea. What life have I woken up to this time, I wonder?*

It was obvious that the most important thing on the desk as far as Charlie Gruff was concerned was a small china plate with three biscuits on it.

Charlie leapt forward and grabbed one but, to Beancat's surprise, didn't stuff it all in his mouth at once. Instead, he held the biscuit in his filthy fingers and nibbled at it slowly, making each mouthful last.

He smiled for the first time since Beancat had laid eyes on him.

*Poor little chap*, thought Beancat. *He really is all skin and bone.*

She caught sight of a line of framed black-and-white photographs on the wall. All were of rows of station staff and all included the smartly dressed stationmaster, Mr

Robinson, at the front in the middle. In the first picture, he didn't have a moustache. In the second, a small one. The moustache seemed to get gradually bigger and bigger as each year went by and each new photo was taken!

Furry Purry Beancat jumped up on to a shelf of big fat books with Bradshaw's

printed on the fronts. But she wasn't interested in those. She had spotted something in the photos and wanted a closer look. Sure enough, there alongside the stationmaster in all eight of the pictures, was Furry Purry Beancat herself. Starting out as an adorable fluff-ball of a kitten and growing larger and larger and larger into a beautiful fluff-ball of a Furry Purry Beancat! As the stationmaster's moustache grew, so did she!

She purred with pride.

*They must have a photo taken of the station staff every year,* she thought. *And there I am, as beautiful as ever, right next to the stationmaster. He really is my special human. I truly am a railway cat!*

*Not that I can remember a thing . . .*

The stationmaster returned with a cup of tea in one hand and a saucer of milk in the other. He placed the saucer on the floor by the desk. 'There you go, Purry,' he said.

*Thank you,* thought Furry Purry Beancat, jumping down from the shelf. She lapped at the milk.

The stationmaster placed the cup on his desk in front of the boy.

'Fank you,' said Charlie. He seemed unsure whether to take a pause from eating his biscuit to sip his tea, or to carry on eating.

Mr Robinson disappeared again for a moment, reappearing with a cup of tea for himself, before sitting behind his desk.

'Is that your cat?' asked Charlie.

'Yes,' said Mr Robinson. 'As much as anyone can own a cat. Her name is Furry Purry Beancat. This is her station.'

Charlie reached out to stroke her back.

His hand was filthy, but Beancat didn't mind. She could tell that he liked her. He stroked her from neck to tail, nervously at first but gaining confidence and applying more pressure with each stroke.

'S'a good name,' said Charlie. 'She's a good cat. Pretty.'

'She is likely to be the most beautiful cat you'll ever lay eyes on,' said the stationmaster proudly. 'And one of the smartest.' Beancat *purrrrrred*. He took a biscuit and then a bite. 'You can have the last one, Charlie,' he said.

'Fank you, sir,' said the boy, as he took it in his grimy hand.

'Now, why did you steal Mrs Fitzpatrick's bag?' the stationmaster asked gently. 'You

know that the only reason you're not in a cell right now is because she got it back and we decided not to call the constable.'

'You decided, more like,' said Charlie. 'That old—'

'Stop that!' said the stationmaster. 'She was the victim.'

Charlie looked down at his cup of tea guiltily. 'Then why's you being kind to me?' he asked.

'I think that kindness can work as well as punishment to help people change their ways,' said Mr Robinson. 'I can see life's been hard on you and you've had few chances in life, so I'm giving you one.'

At that moment, the door to Mr Robinson's office flew open, without so

much as a knock, and in marched the tip of Mrs Fitzpatrick's nose, followed moments later by the rest of her (including that ridiculous hat of hers) and by a police constable, truncheon in hand.

'Arrest that vagabond!' Mrs Fitzpatrick cried, almost stepping on Furry Purry Beancat's tail.

*'Watch where you're standing!'* said an angry Beancat, but all the woman heard was a threatening hiss.

'He stole my purse and I want it back this instant!'

'I don't know nuffink about no purse,' Charlie protested, leaping to his feet. 'I grabbed the bag is all.'

The constable marched over and

thoroughly searched the boy. There was no sign of a purse.

'See?' said Charlie indignantly. 'You got your bag back, lady, and I didn't have no time to open the bag. I'd only just grabbed it when I were caught.'

'That's true, constable,' Tom the porter told the police officer when, a few minutes later, the stationmaster had called him into his office to give his eye-witness account.

'That's as may be,' said the constable, 'the fact remains that this boy here stole the handbag in the first place!'

'An accomplice! He must have had an accomplice who he passed the purse to without anyone seeing!' Mrs Fitzpatrick insisted

'Were you working with someone, Charlie?' asked the stationmaster.

Charlie said nothing.

'Come on, Charlie. It'd be better for you if you told us everything now rather than later.' Mr Robinson urged.

'Well . . . A man came up to me when I was beggin' and asked me if I wanted to earn some money. I weren't gonna say no, were I?'

'But why snatch a bag off a railway platform?' asked Constable Franklin. 'Far easier to take one in the street.'

'Cos it were her bag –' Charlie pointed at Mrs Fitzpatrick – 'that he wanted. Hers in particular, like.'

'And how could this mysterious man

be sure you'd know what Mrs Fitzpatrick looked like, if he wanted you to steal her bag in particular?' asked the policeman.

*Good question*, thought Beancat.

'He described her to me,' said the boy.

*Good answer*, thought Beancat.

'How did he describe her?'

'Not sure I wanna say,' said Charlie, avoiding Mrs Fitzpatrick's glare.

'Because you've made the whole thing up!' snapped Mrs Fitzpatrick, not very charitably.

'He told me to keep me eyes peeled for an old lady with a great big nose an' a dead bird on 'er 'ead!' he blurted out, good and loud.

*I'd recognize Mrs Fitzpatrick from THAT*

*description*, thought Beancat. She could see that nearly everyone in the room was doing their very *best* not to smile.

Mrs Fitzpatrick herself, however, did NOT look happy.

'This little thief is making it all up,' she snapped, her feather hat now bobbing like a cornered chicken.

'Maybe they knew it contained a

purse with donations in it, ma'am?' Tom suggested reasonably.

'Very few donations,' protested Mrs Fitzpatrick. 'I had only just started calling upon people.'

The constable turned from her to Charlie Gruff. 'Describe the man to me,' he said to the boy, with a no-nonsense voice he was probably taught at police school.

'Tall an' thin. Brown checked jacket an' trousers, and a brown 'at,' said Charlie.

'That sounds like the man who handed your bag back to you, Mrs Fitzpatrick,' cried Tom. 'He would have had the opportunity to reach inside!'

Beancat had been listening intently *and* she could, of course, understand what they

were saying, and she could talk Animal to most other animals. But could humans understand her? No. *Such a pity they're not the brightest of creatures, she thought, or I could tell them what I saw.*

'I've had *quite* enough!' said Mrs Fitzpatrick. 'I want *action.*'

So Constable Franklin took action. 'Thank you for your time, Mr Robinson,' he said. 'And you, Tom.' He nodded in the direction of the porter. He glared down at Charlie. 'As for you, boy, you're coming with me.'

## CHAPTER 3
## FRIEND OR FOE?

**B**eancat quickly and expertly made herself familiar with her new surroundings. Well, they were new to her, this time around! Discovering the name of her station – and she was already thinking of it as hers – was easy enough. There were signs for it everywhere! It was called KIMBLEDOWN.

There were two railway tracks and two platforms, with a footbridge running between them. She'd already investigated both the footbridge and the other platform, and was now back on Platform One, where all the excitement had been, because it was sunnier.

Furry Purry Beancat settled herself underneath a hanging basket of brightly coloured flowers. Soon she had drifted off to sleep, dreaming of steam engines and whistles and . . . RAIN!

**WOOOAH!** Furry Purry Beancat awoke with a shock. She had cold water on her head and she could hear laughing.

She dashed to one side then turned to look back. Water was dripping from the hanging basket, and Tom the porter was halfway up a short ladder, watering can in hand.

'Ooops! Sorry, Purry!' he laughed.

*You did that on purpose!* thought Furry Purry Beancat, though her cat instincts also told her that Tom liked cats in general and her in particular, so he was being mischievous rather than nasty . . . Not that this made A WET HEAD acceptable. She arched her back and hissed at Tom to show her displeasure.

'Sorry, Beancat,' Tom said again, as he came down the ladder with the watering can. But he was still smiling and didn't look particularly sorry! He picked up the ladder, tucked it under his arm and walked away, whistling innocently.

A large black crow landed on the edge of the freshly watered hanging basket, causing it to swing. Beancat thought it a bit of a cheek that the bird didn't seem bothered she was sitting nearby and might easily pounce. Beancat isn't a big fan of birds. Most of them seem to like teasing cats, bobbing and flapping about and being all interesting but never letting themselves be caught. They simply fly away!

'Go away!' she hissed.

'Charming!' said the bird. 'Thanks for that! What's made you such a grump, Beancat?'

*Ooops!* thought Beancat. *He might be a friend.* 'Tom made that hanging basket drip

on me,' she replied. 'That's what.'

The crow laughed: *'Caw! Caw! Caw!'*

'Thanks for that,' said Beancat.

'I heard Polly will be on the 12.27,' said the bird.

'Really?' said Beancat, trying to sound matter of fact but wondering who Polly was.

'You must be pleased,' said the bird.

'Of course I'm pleased!' said Furry Purry Beancat. *Polly must be important to me*, she thought.

When the station clock showed 12.24, a train pulled into the station. A handful of passengers were already on the platform ready to board, and Tom was at the ready with his porter's trolley. Even the nice stationmaster was there.

The train stopped. The engine hissed. Doors to various carriages and compartments opened, and a number of people climbed out. A few were dressed in bright red soldier's uniforms.

Furry Purry Beancat guessed who Polly was at once. Her face was so like the stationmaster's but without the moustache, of course! She had jet-black hair, great big brown eyes and was carrying a dome-shaped birdcage that looked almost as big as she was! She was climbing out of the guard's van at the very back of the train. 'Thank you, Jim!' she said to the guard.

'Look after yourself, Miss Polly.' said Jim Greaves, raising his cap with a great big smile on his face.

Next Polly turned towards the front of the train and shouted, 'Thank you, Jon Tucker!'

Furry Purry Beancat saw an arm stick out from the footplate of the steam engine and wave.

'Thank you, Mr Mason!'

Another hand appeared from the side of the engine. This one was waving a grimy rag.

Now, Polly turned and gave all her attention to the stationmaster on the platform. 'Grandpa!' she shouted with glee as she ran towards him. She placed the cage on the platform and jumped into his arms.

*Aha!* thought Furry Purry Beancat. *I*

*was right.* Her thoughts were interrupted by the thing in the birdcage.

'Hullo, Fatso,' he said.

Beancat looked at him. Whoever he was, whatever he was, he was white and feathery with a funny tuft at the back of his head. And he had big beak. It was even more impressive than Mrs James Fitzpatrick's nose!

'Greetings, Big Beak,' she said. They

obviously knew each other but they were unlikely to be friends, what with him being a bird and all, and if he was going to be so rude – *Fatso*, indeed! – then Beancat would be rude right back.

'That's not very polite,' said the bird. 'As you well know, I am a very fine cockatoo.' He gave Beancat a wide-eyed, beaky look.

'And as you well know, I'm very slim under all this beautiful fur,' said Beancat indignantly. It was true.

'And I'm very wise behind all this beak!' said the cockatoo, followed by a screech of what may have been laughter.

The stationmaster laughed. 'It looks like Yorkie and Beancat are having a catch-up conversation, Polly!' he said.

*Ah, Yorkie must be this annoying bird's name*, thought Beancat.

'Is Caw still around, or did that scruffy old crow stick his beak in where it didn't belong once too often?' Yorkie asked Beancat.

*And the crow is actually called Caw!* thought Furry Purry Beancat. *It's very helpful when people just give me this information!* 'Oh, he's still very much around,' she told the bird.

There was a call of 'All aboard!' and the final slamming of carriage doors, then a long blow on a whistle. As the hands on the station clock showed 12.27, the train pulled out of the platform, right on time.

Having greeted her grandfather, Polly

turned to Beancat. She cuddled and stroked her and buried her face deep in her fur. 'Nothing smells as lovely as a sun-warmed Beancat!' she declared. Furry Purry Beancat was purring SO loudly it seemed to block out all the sounds around her!

'I fail to see what's so exciting about a fat-ball of purring fur!' said the cockatoo from his cage.

'Oh, poor Yorkie,' said Polly (who obviously couldn't understand what her bird was actually saying). 'Are you jealous of all the attention I'm giving Purry? I do love you too.'

'Of course you do,' said Yorkie. 'I am extraordinarily loveable.'

Polly opened the door to the cage and Yorkie stuck out his head. She put out her hand and he hopped on to her arm.

Then Yorkie spoke OUT LOUD in English so that Polly could understand him: *'Free at last! Free at last!'* Then made a sound like a bell ting-a-linging.

Beancat was stunned.

'Don't tell me you forgot my party piece?' said Yorkie. 'I'm one talented bird.'

'How could I forget?' asked Beancat.

'And what have you been up to since our last visit?' asked Yorkie. 'Been admiring your own reflection in puddles? Licking your bottom clean?'

'Yorkie's pleased to see you,' said Polly, tickling Beancat under the chin.

*If only you knew what he'd just said!*
thought Furry Purry Beancat. Outrageous!
Polly mistakenly seemed to think she and
Yorkie actually LIKED each other. Well,
there was no chance of THAT!

The cockatoo walked a few talon-paces sideways along Polly's shoulder and then back again.

'Don't you give her shoulder ache, you inconsiderate owl?' asked Furry Purry Beancat.

'I've told you a thousand times. I have hollow bones,' the bird replied. 'And I'll remind you that I'm no owl, what with their tiny little beaks!' He followed this up by squawking, *As light as a feather! As light as a feather!* for Polly to hear and understand.

'As light as a feather? That must be because of your feather-light bird brain!' said Beancat. She was rather enjoying being rude to Yorkie! Perhaps this was how

their conversations usually went?

'Come on, Polly,' said her grandfather. 'Let's go up to the house for lunch and find your grandmother.'

# CHAPTER 4
# ENDING WITH A BANG!

As they walked to the stationmaster's house, they passed a lad selling newspapers. He was waving one in the air, shouting, 'Fears of war grow stronger! Prime minister to make statement tomorrow! Fears of war grow stronger! Prime minister to—'

His cries were cut short as they entered the house. 'Grandma?' Polly cried.

'Polly! You're here!' Mrs Robinson ran to give her granddaughter a hug. She had grey hair tied neatly in a bun, and wore a brown skirt and a white blouse with a frilly front, and a cameo brooch just below her neck. 'Come, let's have some tea,' she said, and ushered them into the kitchen.

As she set out tea for her husband and granddaughter, Mrs Robinson gave Furry Purry Beancat a bowl of milk, and a good stroke from head to the tip of the tail once she'd placed it on the floor. Yorkie was given some nuts, and he managed to send bits of shell flying all over the place when he cracked them open with his beak.

'WHAT A MESS! WHAT A MESS!' he cackled out loud in Human English and then made his ting-a-ling sound again.

'Oh, Yorkie!' said Polly, scuttling around to pick up the pieces.

Polly's grandma laughed. 'Don't worry, Polly!' she said. 'We're all used to Yorkie's table manners by now.'

'Or lack of them,' muttered Beancat between laps of milk.

The stationmaster looked around the kitchen. 'The gang's complete,' he said.

'Not quite,' said Mrs Robinson. 'Where's Caw?'

'At the window, of course!' Polly grinned and, sure enough, there was the crow, tapping at the glass above the kitchen sink with his beak.

'Quite extraordinary!' said the stationmaster. 'I don't think that chap will ever forget what you did for him.'

*What DID you do for him?* Beancat wondered.

Polly had, meanwhile, crossed over to the window, stood on a stool, leaned across the sink and opened it.

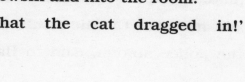

'*Caw!*' said Caw in thanks. He hopped off the windowsill and into the room.

'Look what the cat dragged in!' said Yorkie.

Watching everything with fresh eyes, Beancat found the whole scene fascinating: a granddaughter with a pet cockatoo visiting a stationmaster and his wife, joined by a tame crow and a VERY purry, furry – and very beautiful – station cat!

'Now,' announced Grandma, 'it's time for lunch!'

Time passed quickly and evening came. Beancat had taken the opportunity to explore the house from attic to coal cellar. She'd found her thoughts returning again and again to Charlie Gruff, locked up at the police station. And to Brown Bowler

and the purse he'd stolen from Mrs James Fitzpatrick.

She wandered into the dining room. Polly was sitting, cross-legged, on a round rug by an unlit coal fire, reading a book. Mrs Robinson was sitting in a comfy chair, one side of the rug, knitting. The stationmaster was sitting in another comfy chair on the other side of the rug, snoring gently.

Furry Purry Beancat went over to investigate Polly's book.

She was surprised to see the girl's name on the cover. She blinked her beautiful big green eyes and pushed her little pink nose a little closer. What a surprise Polly would have had if she knew that Beancat was reading the title.

Yorkie, meanwhile, was sitting on the swing-perch in his cage on a round oak table, his big beak sticking through the cage's open door. Beancat jumped on to the table beside him. She made it look easy. There seemed to be no judging of height or distance. She simply jumped up and landed perfectly.

She had a question and, though she'd rather not be asking a bird, none of the humans would understand a meow when they heard it. 'Why does Mrs Fitzpatrick have a man's name when she's a woman?' Furry Purry Beancat asked.

'What are you on about, fleabag?'

'Why is she called James?'

Yorkie gave a screech of laughter. (Then he mimicked the sound of a bell again. Cockatoos are very good at impersonating noises.) The stationmaster sat bolt upright in his chair and fumbled for his fob watch in his waistcoat pocket. Then he muttered something, put it away again and quickly went back to dozing.

His wife chuckled to herself.

'I'd forgotten how forgetful you can be, Purry!' said Yorkie. 'Mrs James Fitzpatrick isn't called James. That's the name of

her husband, Major Fitzpatrick. The one in charge of the regiment of soldiers based over in Bracken. It's like Mrs Jack Robinson –' He nodded his head in the direction of Polly's grandma – 'is actually called Martha.'

*That doesn't seem fair,* thought Beancat. She wondered whether Queen Victoria had a husband and, if so, whether he had to be called by HER first name. That would be funny. *But, then again, the world isn't fair,* she thought. *Like poor Charlie, having to beg and even steal, just to be able to eat.*

After supper, the stationmaster announced, 'I think I'll stroll back down to the station with Beancat for my last look-around of the day.'

'Do you think Mrs Fitzpatrick will press charges?' asked Martha, as her husband got to his feet.

'I rather think it's gone beyond that,' said the stationmaster. 'It's charity donations – other people's money – that was stolen, so it's become an even more serious matter.'

Polly's grandma shook her head sadly. 'Mrs Fitzpatrick is one of the least charitable people I know! Her husband is the soldier with all those men under his command, yet he's the kind one and she's the one who barks orders at everyone! It's all show with her. It's more about being *seen* to be charitable and good rather than actually caring about people.'

'Now, now,' said Mr Robinson.

Yorkie hopped up into Martha Robinson's

lap and looked at her with his big, beady birdy eyes. *'Love me. I'm adorable!'* he said, loud and clear in Human-speak.

They all laughed.

Polly's grandma gently stroked his feathered head. 'We do, Yorkie,' she said with a chuckle.

*Speak for yourself,* thought Beancat.

The stationmaster and Furry Purry Beancat walked side by side towards the station.

*So I don't sleep in their house but at the station itself,* she thought. *I truly am the station cat!*

When they arrived, they went into the ticket office. 'Evening, Barnes,' the stationmaster said to the ticket clerk.

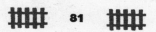

Beancat sniffed the ticket-office air with her little pink nose. Barnes smelled of cheese sandwiches. She looked around. *Bread crumbs.*

'Evenin', sir,' said Barnes. 'There was a telephone call for you from Major Fitzpatrick, not five minutes since. He asks that you telephone him at your earliest convenience.'

'Thank you. Did he say what it was about?'

'No, sir. Other than it were important.'

Telephones were a rarity back in Queen Victoria's day. Very few homes or offices had them. People usually sent important messages by telegram. These started out as a handwritten messages on forms.

They were then turned into Morse code (electronic dots and dashes) and sent down telegraph wires. At the other end, they were turned back into words, printed, put in envelopes and delivered as telegrams.

The reason why the major had such a new-fangled device as a phone was because he was in charge of so many soldiers. And the station? Because so many trains and passengers had to pass that way, including troops.

But Beancat didn't know all this and, even if she had, she was otherwise occupied.

She'd moved on from sniffing cheese-sandwich crumbs and was now looking around in wonder. There was the little ticket-office counter with its glass window

through which Barnes could dispense tickets to the travelling public and, to the right, mounted on the wall were column after column of railway tickets, one stacked on top of the other, divided into different colours. There were rubber stamps and timetables.

That was one of the great things about being a cat. You got to see behind the scenes! Furry Purry Beancat looked around. *Do I have a cat basket in here?* she wondered.

Mr Robinson unlocked the door to his office and hurried inside; Beancat followed. He closed the door behind them and picked up a strange device and spoke into it.

'Operator, get me Major Fitzpatrick at Bracken Barracks, please,' he said.

'Barrowhill 4545.'

He was soon connected.

With her super-swivelling satellite-dish-style cat ears, Furry Purry Beancat could easily hear both ends of the conversation, but she was only half listening.

'Mr Robinson?'

'Yes, major?'

'Thank you for calling me back.'

'Nothing urgent, I hope?'

'If you consider a crate of **dynamite** going missing from the armoury urgent, then it's urgent, Mr Robinson.'

'Dynamite?'

At the word 'dynamite', Furry Purry Beancat suddenly became alert.

'Yes. You know, TNT. Explosives. Big bang and whatnot.'

'I . . . I see.'

'Probably nothing to worry about, but if it has been stolen, the thief may try to move it by train. You haven't seen anything suspicious, have you?'

'No . . . No, major.'

'No one breaking into a cold sweat,

lugging an outsized suitcase?'

'No, major.'

'Well, do keep an eye out and report anything suspicious straight to me. There's a good chap.'

'I will,' the stationmaster assured him. 'I certainly will.' He put down the telephone and stroked Beancat between the ears. 'Well, the major is certainly a cool customer, Purry!' he said. 'I'd be a lot more worried about missing dynamite than he sounds . . . No, I *am* a lot more worried! Imagine if these explosives have fallen into the wrong hands!'

*First a purse, now dynamite?* thought Beancat. *Whatever will get stolen next?*

# CHAPTER 5
# A SLEIGHT OF HAND

The next day, Beancat was patrolling Platform Two for both purse and dynamite thieves when she heard a familiar voice.

'Hello, you!' said Polly, bending down to gather up Beancat in her arms.

Beancat *purrrrrred* as she looked around

the station from this new position. Her beautiful green eyes widened. There were a few people dotted about the platform – a red-coated soldier, a woman and child, three smartly dressed ladies – but Beancat's attention was on a tallish man wearing a green suit.

It looked to Beancat like the suit had seen better days; that it had once been expensive and rather fine, but now looked lived-in and a little worse for wear. The man was clean-shaven and wearing a green top hat.

But it wasn't the *clothes* that interested Furry Purry Beancat. In fact, when she'd seen him the previous day he'd been dressed differently. He'd had a moustache

back then, too, because the man in the green suit was none other than Brown Bowler, the purse thief! She would bet her little pink nose on it. And her little pink nose was VERY good at identifying people – as well as the remains of cheese sandwiches – by their smell.

A train pulled into the platform, coming to a halt with a hiss of steam. Smoke from the engine's funnel filled the air. Some people got off the train while others climbed aboard. There was hustling and bustling and bustling and hustling. Brown Bowler (now top-hatted and in green) appeared to be looking for a particular compartment in a particular carriage. He opened the door and stepped inside. There was nothing for it, Beancat would have to follow him! She leapt out of Polly's arms and in through the door after him.

*Let's see what you get up to next*, she thought.

'Wait! WAIT!' called Polly, leaping into the carriage after her.

Doors were slammed. The whistle blew and off they chugged.

Furry Purry Beancat found herself in a compartment with heavily padded bench seats on either side, facing each other, each with a mirror and a luggage rack above them. At the opposite end of the compartment were two internal windows and a sliding door which led on to a corridor running the length of the carriage.

There were already five people in the compartment, designed to seat six, which meant that Polly had no choice but to sit between Brown Bowler, who was by the window, and a woman dressed from head to toe in black. She eyed Furry Purry Beancat as the cat jumped up on to Polly's lap.

*Cat hairs*, thought Beancat. *She's worried I'll cover her in cat hairs!*

Directly opposite Brown Bowler was someone reading a newspaper – another headline about the worries of war. Furry Purry Beancat couldn't see the person's face, just their gloved hands holding the paper, and their trousers from the knees down and their black shoes. They were beautifully polished.

Beancat could tell that the remaining two people in the carriage were together, even before they spoke. An elderly couple, they both seemed to have a light dusting of powder on them! It was flour! Furry Purry Beancat wondered if it meant that they were bakers!

The person hidden behind the newspaper remained hidden behind the newspaper.

*Must be reading a very interesting piece of news,* thought Beancat.

A few minutes later, the sliding door leading to the corridor opened and a man in a railway uniform stepped into the compartment.

'Tickets, please!' he said, touching the peak of his cap in respect to the passengers. He saw Beancat and the girl. 'Hello, Miss Polly,' he said, looking at her special ticket. 'Hello, Purry.'

'Hello, Mr Gunn,' Polly replied with a big grin.

Furry Purry Beancat purred loudly.

The person behind the newspaper lowered it at last, revealing himself to be an elderly looking gentleman. He had a shock of white hair and wrinkles on his face, and a pair of round glasses perched on the end of his nose.

*He smells a bit strange*, thought Beancat. But it was his eyes that really caught Furry Purry Beancat's attention. He had the lightest blue eyes she had ever seen on a human. The light-blue eyes of a husky dog. Or a wolf. The effect was quite startling.

Without removing a glove, the elderly looking man with the lightest of light-blue eyes began fumbling for his ticket while the railway guard was clipping those of the other passengers. Now he pulled it from a waistcoat pocket and handed it to the guard.

'Thank you, sir,' said Harold Gunn, who clipped it and handed it back to him.

The gentleman dropped his ticket with an, 'Oh!'

Brown Bowler – who was now clean-shaven and dressed in green, if you recall – bent down, quick as a flash, picked up the dropped ticket and handed it back to the elderly gent.

At least, that's what he *appeared* to be doing, but that was not what actually happened at all.

Both Furry Purry Beancat and Polly saw what ACTUALLY happened, because Beancat was already keeping a sharp eye on Brown Bowler and because children are FAR more observant than grown-ups!

The gentleman had dropped the ticket, and Brown Bowler had bent down, picked it up, hidden it in the palm of his hand and then handed the gentleman another ticket – or whatever it was. It was like a conjuring trick. They'd done a swap!

*Hmmm,* thought Furry Purry Beancat.

*How very interesting.*

The cogs in that furry purry brain of hers began to whir . . .

*The ticket Blue Eyes gave Mr Gunn must have been a proper ticket, because Mr Gunn inspected it before clipping it with his special metal ticket-clipper. But what would Brown Bowler want with an ordinary, now-clipped, ticket? Nothing, she reasoned. Hmmmm. So it's what Brown Bowler has swapped the ticket **FOR** and **GIVEN** to Blue Eyes that's the important thing. And it must **ALSO** be important that Brown Bowler and Blue Eyes don't look like they know each other, otherwise they wouldn't have needed to do it this way. . .*

Now, of course, Polly knew NONE of this

because she hadn't seen Brown Bowler the day before like Beancat. But she was excited because she loved a mystery and a puzzle, and wondered what was going on!

Moments later, the train was plunged into darkness and Beancat's heart skipped a beat. It took her a moment to realize why it had suddenly turned to night.

*We're in a tunnel!* she thought, as they came out the other side, her little heart beating faster than she cared to admit. *Me, afraid? Never! A silly old railway tunnel, that's all!*

Soon after this, the train slowed and came to a halt. Blue Eyes folded his newspaper and tucked it under his arm, picked up his hat from his lap and stood

up, rather shakily, with the aid of a silver-topped cane. He opened the outer door and stepped down from the carriage on to the platform.

Polly stood up with such speed that Furry Purry Beancat went tumbling from her lap, but landed on all four paws, as cats do. Before the magnificent moggy knew what was happening, Polly had stepped out of the carriage too. She was going to follow Blue Eyes!

*Polly could be in danger without even knowing it!* thought Beancat, and she quickly jumped out on to the platform, too, just before the door closed behind her.

'Did you see that, Purry?' whispered Polly (a little too loudly for Beancat's liking), as they walked side by side. 'That man back there slipped the old man something. I do love a mystery! Let's follow him!'

*But what you don't know is that one of them is the thief who took Mrs Fitzpatrick's purse,* thought Beancat. *We must be very careful!*

Beancat could see a few roads dotted with buildings beyond. The handful of passengers who'd got off the train were leaving through a small gate at the side. Blue Eyes was amongst them, leaning heavily on his silver-topped walking cane. Polly and Furry Purry Beancat followed from a safe distance.

The further they walked from the station, the more nervous Polly became. It

had started out as a bit of a fun – for her, at least – but now she was beginning to wonder if the man might get a bit angry if he found out that they were following him.

Whereas Beancat could stay in full view, jumping from flint garden wall to pavement to footpath – because who would think a beautiful furball such as she would be following them? – Polly had to be careful.

Once on a footpath, the man turned round on a couple of occasions, but Polly was quick to hide, so he didn't so much as catch a glimpse of her. Then Polly and Beancat witnessed an extraordinary transformation. Suddenly, Blue Eyes wasn't leaning on his cane any more. In fact, his legs stopped being so bent at the knee and he walked with the stride of a much younger man, his whole body more upright. He veered off the path into a small patch of trees, which, to Furry Purry Beancat, smelled very much of DOG and other unpleasant things.

Unaware that he was being watched, Blue Eyes reached inside a hole in a hollow tree and pulled out a small case. Then he laid it on the ground and opened it.

What he did next made Furry Purry Beancat's AND Polly's eyes widen in surprise. Having removed his glasses and put them in his breast pocket, he peeled off one of his bushy white eyebrows! He held it in his hand like a rare caterpillar, then dropped it into the open case. He did the same with the second eyebrow. Beancat saw that, in truth, he had two, much thinner, darker eyebrows. Next, off came the shock of white hair. It was nothing more than a wig! Now Blue Eyes was rubbing his face and the wrinkles were coming off in his hands like some kind of rubbery glue!

Polly's eyes grew wider and wider in amazement and her mouth was open like a big letter 'O'.

*No wonder he smelled a bit funny,* thought Beancat. *Those false eyebrows must have been held on with a special glue.*

Five minutes later, the transformation was complete. His clothes might be the same as the old gent he'd pretended to be on the train, but they looked different and less crumpled on this upright, younger fellow.

And off he went. A new man!

# CHAPTER 6
# NOW YOU SEE ME

**B**lue Eyes strode out with the brisk walk of a young man. The path twisted past a churchyard which he entered via a covered, wooden gate and then marched between headstones towards the church itself. As Beancat followed him through the long grass at the fringes of the church yard, staying near the flint wall which surrounded it, Polly crouched behind headstone after headstone, getting closer. There was the hoot of a train whistle in the distance.

*A church?* thought Beancat. *He's going to church?*

Blue Eyes reached the large porch to the south door with built-in wooden benches running down either side but, instead of going in, as Furry Purry Beancat had expected, he kept on walking with purposeful strides.

In a far corner of the churchyard, he finally reached an old wooden gate, covered in ivy and hanging from one hinge, and overhung by trees. At first glance it looked as if the old gate hadn't been opened in years but, carefully moving aside a small, ivy-covered, log in front of it, Blue Eyes pulled it open without so much as a creak, went through the gap and closed it behind him. Furry Purry Beancat could smell the fresh oil on the one remaining hinge.

She looked around. Polly was moving closer, crouching from headstone to rosebush to carved angel, a great big grin across her face.

There was a fluttering of wings. Beancat looked up, distracted.

'*Caw!*' said a voice. 'What's this game?'

'Woah!' said Beancat, glaring at the crow who'd landed on the grass in front of them.

'*Caw!*' said a delighted Polly. 'What are you doing here?'

'Just what I was about to ask,' said Furry Purry Beancat, less than thrilled.

Caw hopped closer to them. 'Spotted you a mile off, I did, Purry,' he said, though to Polly it just sounded like bird chatter. 'Was flying over when I caught sight of that fluffy tail of yours. Enough to put a peacock to shame, it is. Thought I'd swoop down and see where your travels have led you today.'

'Well, you've landed yourself in a proper mystery,' said Beancat. 'We're following a master of disguise who is definitely up to something.' She had a sudden thought! *Bird or not, Caw might be rather useful.* 'Fly over that wall, will you, and tell us what Blue Eyes is up to. Pleeeease.'

'Since you asked so *nicely*,' cawed Caw, and he took flight.

'Fancy seeing him here!' said Polly with a grin.

After a while, Caw returned.

'You're back!' said Polly. She held up a hand and the crow perched on her finger.

'Well?' asked Furry Purry Beancat.

'Very well, thank you,' said Caw. 'What about you?'

'I meant, well, what did you find out?'

'Aha!' said the crow, jumping off Polly's finger and hopping around on the grass like crows do. 'There's an old railway siding over there. An engine shed and all. Doesn't look like it's been used in years. There's a rusted up old steam engine blocking the entrance.'

'And the man we were following?' asked Beancat.

'He was talking to another bloke—'

'Bloke?' asked Beancat.

'Geezer . . . Man,' said Caw.

Polly gave a little chuckle. 'You two

sounded like you were having a proper little conversation,' she said. 'What with all that crowing and meowing!'

If only she knew!

'I'm going to take a closer look,' said Polly, making her way over to the hedge with a strange waddle, still crouched down and bent at the knee. She sounded all excited.

'Did you recognize this other man?' asked Furry Purry Beancat urgently.

'No!' cawed Caw. 'The man you followed – Blue Eyes – took out a small folded piece of paper and handed it to the other man.'

'What colour was it?'

'A sort of pinky colour,' said Caw, tilting

his head to one side and then the other. Crows like to do things like that.

'Railway-ticket pink?' asked Beancat.

'So THAT'S why the colour seemed familiar!' said Caw, mulling things over in his bird brain. 'Precisely that pink! The other man unfolded the paper and there was something inside. I couldn't see what it was at first, so I had to hop closer.'

'Go on!' Furry Purry Beancat insisted. 'What happened next?'

'I perched myself on top of the funnel of the rusty old steam engine and do you know what I saw? Caw!'

'If I knew, we wouldn't be having this conversation,' said the cat, thinking: *Hurry up, you silly old bird, and tell me!*

'It was a coin. A silver coin.' Caws eyes sparkled.

*All this for a COIN?* thought Furry Purry Beancat.

Polly came back over to Beancat. 'There are two of them over there,' she said proudly. 'I saw the man from the train talking to a thin man. I think they're having a secret meeting. Let's go and take a look!'

Beancat wished she could warn Polly that they might be in actual danger, but the poor girl couldn't speak Animal! Before Beancat knew what was happening, Polly had marched up to the churchyard door and was about to turn the big round handle at the exact moment when it started to be pushed open from the other side!!! (Yes,

that's THREE exclamation marks.)

Polly skedaddled behind a rose bush by an enormous grave stone shaped like an obelisk, Beancat lost herself in the hedge and Caw took flight. When Blue Eyes emerged in the churchyard, for it was he, he had no IDEA that he was being followed by the stationmaster's granddaughter, a crow and an extraordinarily beautiful Furry Purry Beancat. He carefully returned the ivy-covered log back to its position in front of the gate and then moved off.

Polly waited until the man had disappeared round the side of the church before coming out of hiding. As quick as a flash, she was over by the gate, rolling the log aside, and pulling it open.

Furry Purry Beancat certainly wasn't going to let Polly face the thin man alone, so she darted between the girl's legs . . .

They found themselves by a railway track, but it was nothing like the tidy and well-cared for track at Kimbledown Station. Here, the trackside was overgrown and some of the sleepers – the great big thick wooden planks lifting the two metal rails off the ground – were missing or shifted out of place. Some of the iron rails themselves were buckled, bent or broken. Tall weeds grew where they shouldn't and there, just as Caw had said, sat a rusty old steam-engine blocking one entrance to a ramshackle engine shed.

*The thin man who Blue Eyes gave a coin*

*to must be in the engine shed*, thought Furry Purry Beancat. She strolled right on in, as though she had every right to be there – as cats do – but, when inside, she found it empty.

Caw swooped down next to Beancat. He'd been surveying the scene from the sky. 'There's no sign of the thin bloke, Furry. He's disappeared into thin air!'

# CHAPTER 7
# NOW YOU DON'T

**P**olly was puzzled. She was a VERY puzzled Polly indeed.

'Where's the other man gone, Beancat?' she said, turning round and round. 'People don't just melt away to nothing.'

*Meow*, Beancat agreed.

'Most mysterious!' said Polly to no one

in particular, having one last, unsuccessful look for the thin man. Apart from the hedge running alongside the churchyard, and clumps of brambles and scrubby plants here and there, there were no trees or bushes for someone to hide behind. 'This must be the old Treybridge Siding,' she said. 'I've heard Grandpa talk about it, but I've never been here! It leads off the main line, but was closed years ago. Something to do with landslides.'

*Landslides?* thought Beancat. I'm sure we would have heard something if the Thin Man had suddenly been buried under a pile of soil!

'Maybe there's a secret passage!' said Polly, excited at the sudden thought of it.

*Unlikely,* thought Beancat. *It's not as if we're in an ancient castle . . .*

Polly started to walk round the inside of the engine shed. The front of it was open so that engines could be driven right in and out on a stretch of railway track leading right inside the building. . . except that now the track was blocked by the rusty old engine and, anyway, the railway siding looked to have been disconnected from the main track for a good few years. There were chunks of rusty pieces of machinery scattered about the place and even some old tools. Grass and weeds grew through the cracks of what was once the engine-shed floor, but now looked to be a mixture of compacted soil, stone slabs and broken concrete. Polly was pressing and twisting and pulling anything and everything that stuck out of the walls to see if there was a knob which might cause a hidden door to swing open.

If Polly had understood Animal, Beancat would have pointed out that, even if one of these knobs *had* caused a door in the wall to spring open, there was only one place it could lead: outside the hut, and all three of them had circled that a few times already!

With a lazy lollop, perfected by cats over millennia, Furry Purry Beancat jumped up on to the old steam engine for a better view, in much the same way that an ancient Egyptian cat might have nipped up the first few feet of a pyramid some 4,000 years ago.

As Beancat landed, there was a loud **CLUNK**. To Polly's amazement, to Caw's amazement and to Beancat's amazement, a large stone slab on the ground, just

inside the entrance to the shed, lifted up
like the lid to a jack-in-the-box.

'Cool!' said Polly.

*'Caw!'* went Caw.

*'Meow!'* went Furry Purry Beancat.

CLUNK!

An old spanner and bolt had been sitting on the slab, but now that it had revealed itself as a hatch door, Beancat saw that both items were actually attached to it! The entrance had been very well disguised by someone.

'You found it, Furry!' said Polly. 'What a clever cat!'

'Huh!' cawed Caw. 'It was a fluke!'

'Says who?' asked Beancat, trying out her of-course-I-knew-what-I-was-doing-all-along expression.

Polly was already hurrying over to the entrance to the secret passage.

*The thin man might still be down there*, thought Furry Purry Beancat. *If Polly goes first, who knows what might happen?* With that in mind, she launched herself off the

old steam engine and dived through the gap before anyone could stop her. Moments later, Polly had also made her way through the hole in the ground.

'Good luck, Beancat!' Caw cawed. There was no way he – a bird – was going down any secret passage. He was used to wide-open skies. 'What shall I do?'

'Something useful!' Beancat called back.

'Such as?' called Caw.

But Beancat was already too far down the tunnel to hear.

The passage seemed old. Ancient, even. Certainly much older than the engine shed itself. Some of it was clearly cut through solid rock. Where the original passage-makers had hit soil, they'd built stone walls, which, in some places, had been repaired with patches of brickwork which also looked very old. These were much smaller than the bricks with which the stations were built. The ceiling was timbered in places, with stone or brick between the rafters.

Somehow, there was natural light in the passage; not much, but enough not to need flaming torches attached to the wall. And Beancat could smell fresh(ish) air. The original builders must have created clever openings above at various intervals to let in daylight and outside air.

*And someone has kept those openings unblocked*, thought Beancat. *This is all MOST curious.*

They were going down, down, down. In some places, the floor of the secret passage sloped. In other places, there were stone steps, worn with age.

*What can this have been used for?* Beancat wondered. *Where does it lead?*

'Isn't this EXCITING?' said Polly. 'I can't believe it. I've found my very own, real-life secret passage! None of my friends will believe me!'

Beancat sniffed the air. She smelled soot and damp bricks. She suspected that they must be getting nearer the railway line.

Of course a human's sense of smell was nothing compared to Beancat's (which in turn was NOT as good as a dog's, which is about sixty times better than a person, not that Beancat would ever admit that a dog could beat her on ANYTHING), which was why it was around a minute or so later that Polly excitedly said, 'I smell trains! I wonder if we'll come out through a secret door in Barrowhill Station?'

Beancat doubted it. She guessed all the stations would have been built hundreds of years after this secret passage, but the smell of soot was getting stronger. They reached a series of steps about the length of the staircase back at the stationmaster's house. These were recent and made of wood with a wooden handrail. Beancat could smell whatever it was the wooden timbers had been treated with. The nails had yet to be dulled with time. At the bottom was the clear outline of a door.

She was relieved. They'd travelled the length of the secret passage without

encountering the Thin Man. Polly was safe . . . in the passage, at least. Beancat purred, running to the bottom of the stairs, tail held high.

Polly skipped after her, reached up and turned the handle. The door was metal and it made a GR-GR-GRAUNCHING sound as it opened.

They were in a railway tunnel!

'This must be Barrowhill Tunnel!' said Polly. 'Grandpa said it's supposed to be haunted, with lots of unexplained ghostly noises and comings and goings in the night,' said Polly, full of excitement. She gave a ghostly howl, 'WOOOOAHHHH! What a day!' She jumped up in the air and – DISASTER! – she somehow lost her footing and fell backwards with a shriek.

Polly landed awkwardly on one of the two railway tracks. 'Ah! My ankle!' she yelped. She tried to sit up but let out a terrible cry and grabbed her left leg.

Furry Purry Beancat ran over to her, her four legs elegantly stepping over the rails

without a moment's thought. She rubbed her furry body against Polly's tear-stained face.

'Aaaah! This is bad,' said Polly. 'Really bad! I should never have followed that silly man and made you come with me! I'm so sorry, Purry. If only you could understand me!'

*Of course I can understand you,* meowed Beancat desperately. *It's you who can't understand ME!*

Fighting back her sobs, Polly hugged Furry Purry Beancat. 'This is serious, Purry! Really serious. Grandpa told me it's safe to travel the trains. I know the guards, and the drivers and the stokers and the ticket collectors, and lots of other people too.' She paused and tried to sit up. She

let out another yelp of pain and lay back down across the line. 'B-B-But he told me to never ever, ever play, or even step, on the lines themselves . . .'

*And now you're lying across the line and can't move!* thought Beancat.

Polly burst into uncontrollable sobs.

Furry Purry Beancat tried licking Polly's salty tears with her rough, cat tongue. But that wasn't enough. Comforting her friend was important, but not as important as keeping her safe.

She began to concentrate on her surroundings. She swivelled her ears. They picked a slow, steady *drip-drip-drip* of water dripping from the roof. Then there was a scurry of mice.

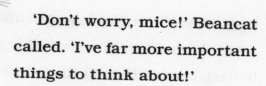

'Don't worry, mice!' Beancat called. 'I've far more important things to think about!'

'She could be lying!' shouted one mouse to another.

'It might be a trap!' cried another.

'Suit yourselves,' said Beancat, 'but I'm not a mouser.'

'She's very fluffy!' cried a third, wanting to be a part of the conversation. There was a giggle and more scurrying around in the dark.

'No peace today!' said one of them. 'It's been like Clapham Junction in here!'

Beancat looked at the door she and Polly

had come through. It wasn't disguised to look like brickwork, or anything like that. It wasn't made to look like something else. It wasn't hidden. It was a metal door, that's all. Simply a door in the wall of the tunnel.

On it was stencilled three words:

# DANGER
# KEEP OUT

which would be enough to keep all but the most inquisitive railway worker out and, anyway, probably very few people entered the tunnel except for track inspection and repairs.

Beancat's blood ran cold. There might be few people who came here. But trains? There would be plenty of trains. And one might be along at any minute.

She dashed over to Polly again to look at her twisted leg and ankle.

And then everything turned from bad to worse.

Not only was poor Polly lying on the track unable to move, but Beancat now noticed that there were things attached to the sides of the rails.

They looked like large candles but these 'candles' were red and had writing on them.

She put her little pink nose right up

close to one and studied the single word:
**DYNAMITE.**

# CHAPTER 8
# NOW YOU'RE TALKING

Furry Purry Beancat was not one to panic. At least, she assumed she wasn't. Maybe she panicked all over the place in some or all of her other eight lives, but she wasn't about to let herself panic today.

There was no way that she could help Polly get off the line, so the most important thing to do first – dynamite or no dynamite – was to stop any trains. Now, which direction did the trains travel on this track, rather than the other one?

*Think, Beancat, think!* she told herself, trying to remember their earlier journey through the tunnel.

They weren't far from one end, so Furry Purry Beancat dashed down the track to take a look.

'Don't leave me!' Polly cried out.

*I'm sorry*, thought Furry Purry Beancat, I really am. But I'm trying to save your life!

The opening was a rather grand stone-fronted brick archway cut into a hillside with grass and trees above. Fixed to the stonework, at human-eye level, was a metal

sign, with a painted white background and raised black letters which read: BARROWHILL TUNNEL.

Beancat looked around desperately. *How can a cat stop a train?* she wondered. Maybe she would panic, after all. She swished her tail.

'*Caw!*' went a familiar voice up above. '*Caw!*'

Furry Purry Beancat looked up. Her big green eyes widened when she saw who was with the crow: a rather exhausted-looking Yorkie.

Beancat had never been so happy to see anyone in her life – well, this life, at least – as she was to see those two.

The crow and the cockatoo flew down to her at the tunnel entrance.

'What are you doing here?' asked Beancat.

'You asked me to do something useful,' said Caw, 'so I got Yorkie and we came to see if we could spot where you and Polly came out of the secret passage!'

'Where is my Polly?' asked Yorkie. 'I'm not used to all this flying. Bad for my feathers, I expect—'

Furry Purry Beancat quickly told them everything.

Before she'd even finished, Yorkie had

flown into the tunnel to find his beloved Polly.

'Oh, Yorkie!' said the girl in amazement, crying out in pain as she tried to move. 'How did you get here?'

At the mouth of the tunnel, Beancat and Caw were deep in conversation.

'Which way do the trains go on this track?' she asked.

'Towards Kimbledown Station,' said Caw. 'Towards home. What are we going to do? What are we going to do?'

'You're going to fly up and see if any trains are heading this way!' said Beancat. 'Be quick!'

And Caw was. The great thing about being a bird was that he had a bird's-eye

view of everything. He could fly in the air and look at all the roads and railway tracks down below. He returned to Beancat.

'The bad news is that there is a train coming this way,' said Caw. '*Caw!* The good news is that it's loading up with soldiers at the station at Bracken Barracks – it must be a special train, laid on just for troops – which means it's still a fair distance away.'

*The dynamite!* thought Beancat. *What if someone knew the troops were coming through this tunnel and planned to blow up the train? With all this talk of war, maybe Brown Bowler, Blue Eyes and the Thin Man are spies! Maybe . . .*

And suddenly a plan popped into her

head. 'Get Yorkie!' she said.

Caw swooped into the tunnel and moments later he returned with Yorkie.

'We can't leave her—'

'Listen, featherbrain,' said Furry Purry Beancat. 'We don't have much time. How do you say those words which people understand?'

'Polly teaches them to me. She says them again and again until I get them right. Or, sometimes, I just listen and imitate them. I can't have conversations or—'

'I need you to say, "Girl in tunnel! Girl in tunnel!"'

'Why not say Polly in tunnel?' asked Caw.

'Because they might think Polly is a parrot' said Beancat, remembering the

*Pretty Polly!* book Polly had been reading with a parrot on the cover. 'Now, can you say it, Yorkie?'

'I can try,' said Yorkie. He marched up and down one of the rails and practised and practised and practised. The words started off sounding strange and a bit wrong. This was the first time he'd had to form a sentence of his own without having a human teach him. He was doing his best!

Caw, meanwhile, had flown back up to check on the progress of the troop train. It was now full AND ON THE MOVE.

When he returned, Yorkie greeted him with a *'Grill in funnel! Grill in tunnel!'*

'Nearly,' said Caw. 'Keep practising!' He hopped over to Beancat. 'I suppose you're going to get him to fly to the troop train and try to speak to the engine driver, Purry?'

'It's our only hope!' said Beancat.

'But why should they believe a bird? They might think he's speaking gibberish. It's not like one human talking to another!'

'There's no time for another plan,' said Beancat. 'If we were humans, we could stand on the track or wave a flag or block the rails . . . but we're just two birds and a cat.'

'If only I could DO something,' cawed Caw.

'You're doing EVERYTHING,' said Beancat. 'It was you who brought Yorkie. It's you who's watching the trains. Now, where's Yorkie?'

'*Girl in tunnel! Girl in tunnel!*' squawked Yorkie.

'Right!' said Furry Purry Beancat, trying to sound more confident that she felt. 'We're as ready we'll ever be.'

They heard another yelp of pain from Polly.

The man driving the 11.17 special train from Bracken Barracks Station that morning was none other than Jon Tucker, the same train driver who'd driven the train which had brought Polly and Yorkie – along with many other passengers – to Kimbledown the day before. The same stoker, Muscles

Mason, was with him on the footplate too, stoking the engine with coal.

They'd just passed through Barrowhill Station, slowing but not stopping, when a big-beaked bird flew on to the footplate and landed directly on the engine controls in front of them. It looked sooty, hot and flustered. Its usually colourful beak was covered in streaks of black.

The two men looked at each other and laughed. 'Seems we have a non-paying passenger!' said Jon Tucker above the noise of the engine.

'I'll bet young Polly Robinson will be wondering where you's got to, Yorkie!' said Muscles Mason.

'*Girl in funnel!*' said Yorkie. '*Grill in*

tunnel! *Girl in tunnel! Grill in funnel! Girl in tunnel!'*

The stoker laughed again but Jon Tucker, the driver, looked serious. 'What if—? No, surely not . . .' He looked ahead. He could see the opening to the tunnel a fair distance up ahead. But a slight movement caught his eye.

There was something on the track, draped over the outer rail, midway between the train and the tunnel. Not a girl but . . . but a cat, looking all floppy and injured. He could just make out a beautiful white tummy.

'That's Furry Purry Beancat!' he cried in amazement and, without a moment's hesitation, he jammed on the brakes.

The engine wheels locked in position but,

at the speed they'd been going and with the weight of the troop-filled carriages behind them, the train kept moving down the track towards Beancat. Fortunately for her, in truth, she was fine and dandy and could get up and leap out of the way if needs be, but she wanted the driver out of the train and on the track – to see what was wrong – so she would stay put if she could.

The locked wheels screeched forward on the metal rails, sparks flying.

'Girl in tunnel! Grill in funnel! Girl in funnel! Girl in tunnel! Girl in tunnel! Girl in tunnel!' squawked Yorkie, who hadn't stopped talking throughout.

Jon Tucker jumped down on to the track. At the far end of the train, Jim Graves the guard jumped down from a carriage. They all walked towards Beancat, who now flipped over on to her front and got nimbly to her feet.

'What—' began Tucker. Then he heard a cry. Not from the cockatoo. More in the distance. It was faint but amplified by the tunnel.

'Help!' it went. 'Help!'

'That's Polly!' said Jim Graves the train guard, coming up alongside him. 'I'd know that girl's voice anywhere!'

Yorkie had left the engine and was now circling above them.

'*Grill in funnel! Girl in tunnel!*' he screeched.

Jon Tucker turned to the train guard.

'Things are getting mighty strange around here!' he said, hurrying down the track towards the tunnel. 'Don't worry, Polly!' he shouted at the top of his lungs. 'Help is on its way!'

Furry Purry Beancat sat in the shadows of the tunnel, forgotten, as the rescue took place. She didn't mind one bit. This was just as it should be. She'd played her part. Now it was down to the humans.

Jim Graves had walked in the opposite direction to the tunnel, back past his stationary train and further up the track to warn any on-coming trains to stop.

Jon Tucker had sent a couple of soldiers down the line in the direction of Kimbledown to do the same for trains in the opposite direction. This was before he saw the dynamite.

While he and a soldier put a splint on

Polly's ankle and bandaged it in place, using items from the train's first-aid box, a sergeant was inspecting the explosives.

'I'm not sure how they intended the dynamite to detonate – perhaps it would be triggered by the train on the rails – but I'd like everyone out of here as soon as possible,' he said. 'Then I'll get one of our explosives experts to make the tunnel safe.'

Muscles Mason and the soldier helped Polly to her feet. She was VERY brave and only cried out in pain a few times.

Yorkie landed on her shoulder. *'Girl in tunnel!'* he said proudly.

Polly's jaw dropped. 'What did you say, Yorkie?'

*'Girl in tunnel!'* said Yorkie, and whistled.

'Who taught you to say THAT?' asked Polly in amazement.

'You mean it wasn't you?' said Muscles Mason in surprise. 'I thought you must have trained him to warn us!'

'Warn you?' Polly had NO idea what the engine stoker was talking about.

Mason decided *not* to mention the part about the stationmaster's cat lying on the rail. This was turning out to be one of THE most unusual days in his many years on the railway.

Furry Purry Beancat was curled up at the foot of Polly's hospital bed and no one

was about to ask her to move. Although they hadn't the slightest idea the part the cat called Beancat had actually played in saving the lives of Polly and a train full of soldiers, they knew that she'd been there and that she was a comfort to Polly, which made her enough of a hero in their eyes.

A police officer came to ask Polly LOTS of questions. She was able to describe the

man Beancat thought of as Brown Bowler (though he'd been dressed in green that day, of course); the man with blue eyes, both in his disguise and out of it; and to give a more vague description of the thin man she'd only glimpsed over the hedge. She told the police officer about the switching of the ticket for something else on the train; described where to find the tree where Blue Eyes had hidden his disguise, cane and case; and about finding the secret passage.

Polly's grandma and grandpa were there too. The stationmaster and his wife were relieved that – broken ankle and twisted knee aside – Polly was unharmed. And so was Major James Fitzpatrick. He listened to Polly's story in silence. 'It sounds like an enemy spy-ring to me,' he said.

After a night in the hospital, Polly was allowed home the following day, but insisted that 'home' be back at the stationmaster's house with Granny and Grandpa and Caw and, of course, Furry Purry Beancat. She wanted her and Yorkie to be with everyone who'd been part of her great adventure.

Later that day, Mr Robinson had an unexpected visitor. It was Major James Fitzpatrick from Bracken Barracks.

'Good afternoon, major,' said the stationmaster. 'Do, please, come into the parlour and take a seat.'

'Thank you, Mr Robinson,' said the major, and the two men sat.

Furry Purry Beancat jumped into her special human's lap and he started to stroke her. 'It seems Mistress Beancat wishes to join us if you have no objection?'

'None at all,' said the soldier, with a smile. 'I came here to tell you that Eileen – Mrs Fitzpatrick – has decided to drop all the charges against the Gruff boy.'

Beancat's ears pricked up.

'Charlie Gruff?' asked the stationmaster, straightening in his chair.

'Yes,' said Major Fitzpatrick.

*Why the sudden change of heart?* Beancat wondered.

'I know you expressed an interest in the boy's well-being, and the theft did happen in your station, so I thought it would be a courtesy to let you know,' began the major. Mr Robinson nodded. 'And,' the major continued, 'it was dynamite stolen from my barracks that was going to be used to blow up your railway, so . . .'

'And your troops, Major Fitzpatrick! I can hardly blame you for that!'

The major shook his head. 'A major breach in security, I'm ashamed to say.'

'And the police are happy to let Charlie Gruff go?' asked the stationmaster. 'They're not going to take the matter any further?'

The major nodded. 'They agreed when I said young Gruff would be joining the regiment as a drummer boy, where he'll be clothed, fed and taught discipline.'

'And how does Charlie Gruff feel about that?' asked Mr Robinson.

'He can tell you himself,' said the major. 'He has something to say to you.'

Major James Fitzpatrick left the room, opened the front door and returned with Charlie.

Beancat jumped off the stationmaster's lap and rubbed her furry, purry body against the boy's ankles. She sniffed the air. *You've had a bath!* she thought. *Or three. And your hair's been brushed.*

She was delighted to see that he had on proper clothes; second-hand, but not third- or fourth- or fifth-hand, and clean and ironed. But what pleased Furry Purry Beancat was that Charlie was wearing shoes. No more bare feet for him.

*And what shiny shoes*, thought Beancat,

admiring herself in their reflection.

'I came to say fank you, sir,' said the boy, facing the stationmaster directly. 'Fank you for being kind 'n' for the biscuits and the tea an' that. And for bein' nice an' tryin' to 'elp me.'

'I'm glad things worked out for you, Master Gruff,' said the stationmaster, getting to his feet. 'It was very kind of Mrs Fitzpatrick to drop the charges like she did.'

'I fink that was more to do with the major than—' Charlie stopped. 'Yes, proper kind,' he said.

Furry Purry Beancat's special human put out his hand and Charlie shook it, man to man.

'Can I stroke Furry Purry Beancat now?' asked Charlie.

'You remembered her name,' said Mr Robinson. 'With all that's happened to you these past few days, I'm impressed.'

*As if he'd forget MY name*, thought Beancat, and was on the receiving end of some very fine head-to-tail stokes from a much cleaner hand this time.

When the two visitors had gone, the stationmaster went to tell Polly's grandma about what had happened to Charlie, and Beancat went to have a chat with Yorkie and Caw. Caw was on the outside ledge of the window deliberately left open for him, pecking a piece of bacon rind, while Yorkie – enormous beak and all – was perched on the arm of a nearby chair. There were nutshells scattered on the carpet all around him.

They talked about nothing in particular for a while, then Beancat said, 'Do you know what?'

'What?' cawed Caw.

'What?' asked Yorkie.

'I'm so proud that you two are my feathery friends,' she said. 'You've proved to me that being a bird is a very special thing.'

'So we're not just bird brains!' said Caw. *'Caw! Caw!'*

*'Grill in funnel!'* said Yorkie proudly. 'It was thanks to your cat brain that my Polly is safe, though, Purry,' he added. 'I'll never forget that.'

*But I will*, thought Furry Purry Beancat. *I won't remember any of this*. And, after that, she purred and padded off. And this is why she didn't get to know what happened next. How the police discovered that Blue Eyes, an enemy spy, had found out important secrets at Bracken Barracks and had hidden his report in a coded message in a hollow coin. How that hollow coin had accidentally been given to the major's wife as a charity donation, so Brown Bowler had had to find a way to steal it back and get it back to Blue Eyes on the train, to pass on to the Thin Man, as originally planned. And how, with the descriptions and information Polly gave them, along with clues they found in the tree and tunnel, all three men were eventually arrested and put in prison and the enemy spy-ring disbanded.

But, for Furry Purry Beancat, the most important thing about the whole adventure was that Polly was safe and on the mend.

*And, for that, I think I deserve a little snooze,* thought Beancat.

She found a patch of sunlight, followed her tail round in a circle three times, then settled herself down in a furry ball of purry cat. She yawned, lowered her head to the ground and pulled her beautiful, fluffy tail in front of her little pink nose.

*Where will I wake up next?* she wondered, closing her big green eyes and drifting off to sleep . . .

# THE REAL
# FURRY PURRY BEANCAT

**PHILIP ARDAGH** didn't have a pet as a child, except when looking after the class tadpole one weekend. He was in his twenties when he got his very first pet, a long-haired tabby-and-white cat called Beany. 'I loved her to bits!' he said. 'She was very furry and very purry!' Beany lived into her eighteenth year and, in creaky old age, sat with Philip in his study as he wrote. One day, it occurred to him that – if he slightly skewed the meaning of a cat having nine lives – she could have

eight other exciting lives ... and the idea of **THE NINE LIVES OF FURRY PURRY BEANCAT** was born.